S0-AQC-513

Big Ride for Little Bear

Retold by Mary C. Olson
Illustrated by Joan Allen

Workbook Activities by Betty Glennon, B.S., M.S., Series Consultant

To the Parent

A love of books and good reading habits both begin at home -- from the picture books you shared with your child as a baby to the read-aloud stories he or she continues to enjoy.

Now your son or daughter is beginning to recognize words and read independently! Encouraging your child to read at home will help build confidence and enthusiasm for a skill he or she will use for a lifetime.

Here are some suggestions to help your beginning reader: Be sensitive to your child's abilities. Do not force your child, particularly if he or she is not yet learning to read in school.

- Be patient for 5 seconds so your child can try to sound out an unfamiliar word.

- Have your child skip an unknown word and read the rest of the sentence. Come back to the word and ask, "What word would make sense here?" Talk about it a little.

- Encourage your child to use any phonics skills that have been learned to help say the word, for example; beginning consonant sounds.

- Praise the effort!

- If a word is still unknown, say it for your child so he or she can continue reading.

- Encourage your child to use pictures as clues to words and meanings.

- Occasionally, before turning a page, ask your child to predict what will happen next. Praise his or her creative thinking.

- Help your child relate the story to his or her own experiences.

Copyright ©1987, 1969 by Western Publishing Company, Inc.
All rights reserved.

Big Ride for Little Bear is adapted from the Golden Beginning Reader, Tiny Bear and His New Sled, by Ruthanna Long.

GOLDEN®, GOLDEN & DESIGN®, and GOLDEN STEP AHEAD & DESIGN® are trademarks of Western Publishing Company, Inc.

A GOLDEN® BOOK
Western Publishing Company, Inc.
Racine, Wisconsin 53404
No part of this book may be reproduced or copied in any form without written permission from the publisher. Produced in U.S.A.

Little Bear had a new sled.
"I need snow for my new sled,"
said Little Bear.

A snowflake fell on Little Bear's nose.
"Snow!" said Little Bear.
"Here is the snow for my new sled."

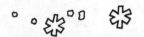 "Little Bear, it is time for our big nap,"
said Mother Bear.
"Bears go to bed when the snow comes."

"I do not want to go to bed,"
said Little Bear.
"I want to ride on my new sled."

"Well, you may take one ride,"
said Mother Bear.
"Then come to bed."

"I will go to the top of Big Hill
and ride down," said Little Bear.
"Then I will go to bed."

Little Bear met a rabbit.
"May I go for a ride on the sled?"
said the rabbit.

"Hop on," said Little Bear.

Little Bear met a squirrel.
"That looks like fun,"
said the squirrel.
"May I ride too?"

"Hop on," said Little Bear.

It was not fun to pull the sled up Big Hill.

At last Little Bear
was at the top of Big Hill.

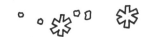

"Now we will go down the hill,"
Little Bear said.
"This will be fun!
Here we go!"

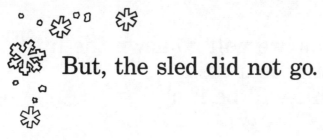 But, the sled did not go.

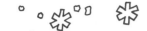 "We want to ride down Big Hill,"
said the squirrel.
"Make the sled go," said the rabbit.

Little Bear said,
"Get off and push.
Then the sled will go."

They all got off.
They gave the sled a push.
"Hop on fast,"
said Little Bear.

"Here we go," they said.
"The sled is fast,"
said the rabbit.
"This is fun!"
said the squirrel.
"I like to ride down Big Hill,"
said Little Bear.

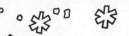

"That was fun!" said the squirrel.
"I want to go down the hill again,"
said the rabbit.
"You may ride on my sled,"
said Little Bear.
"But it is time for my big nap."

 Good Night!

GOLDEN
STEP AHEAD®

Big Ride for Little Bear

Copyright ©1987 Western Publishing Company, Inc.
All rights reserved.

Draw a circle around the name of each picture.

 red sled bed	**1** one on out	 nose out nap
 fill bill hill	❄ sled snow said	 bat bear bed
 pull bull pal	 bill bad bed	 run rabbit ride

<u>Skill:</u> vocabulary review - sled, hill, pull, one, snow, bed, nose, bear, rabbit   1

Draw a line under the sentence that will go with the picture.

They like to ride.

They like to run.

Little Bear hops.

Little Bear naps.

Snow fell on his nose.

This sled is fast.

Little Bear sat down.

They gave the sled a push.

2

<u>Skill:</u> choosing main idea sentences for pictures

1. Little Bear had a ride on
   the new sled.   Yes   No

2. Mother said, "I do not want
   to go to bed."   Yes   No

3. Little Bear pulled a
   dog up Big Hill.   Yes   No

4. It was fun to ride
   down Big Hill.   Yes   No

5. Little Bear went to
   bed after the ride.   Yes   No

Look at the pictures. Read the words. Draw a line from a word in a yellow box to a word in a pink box to make a sentence.

	Mother Bear	hops.
	Rabbit	helps.
	Squirrels	ride.
	Little Bear	fell.
	Snow	naps.

Skill: combining nouns and verbs to form simple sentences.

Draw a line to match the words which have opposite meanings.

up

little

big

out

in

off

on

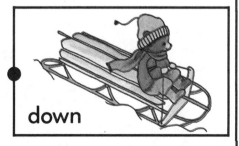

down

Draw lines to match the rhyming words.

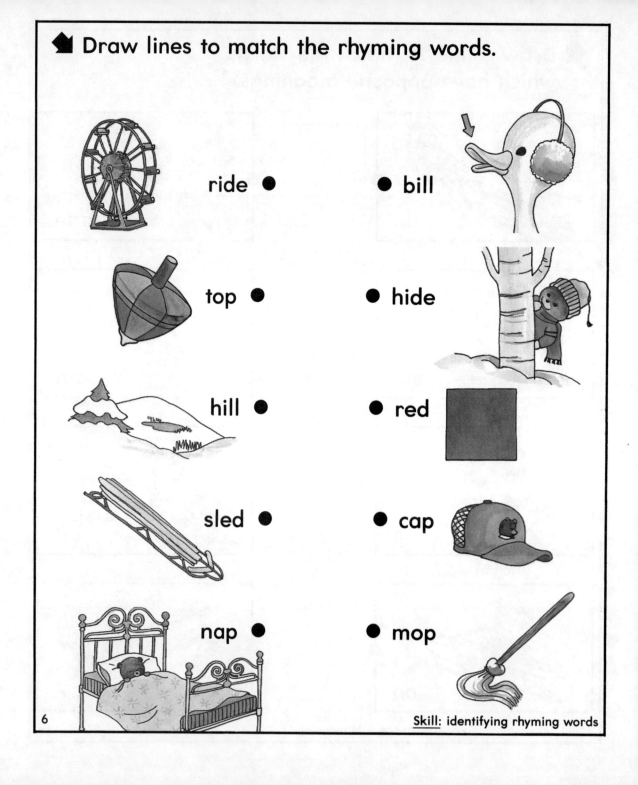

ride •   • bill

top •   • hide

hill •   • red

sled •   • cap

nap •   • mop

6

Draw a circle around the right word to finish each sentence. Write the word on the line.

Little Bear had a _____ .

said
sled
snow

You may take one _____ .

look
go
ride

Can I _____ too?

snow
go
fun

We will go down the _____ .

hill
hat
bear

Skill: using context clues to complete sentences

7

Look at the pictures. Think about the
story. Make an X on the picture
that happened first.

1.

 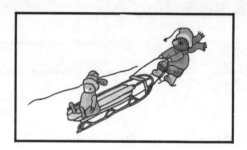

2.

3.

Skill: sequencing events